Christmas Cricket

Christmas Cricket

by Eve Bunting • Illustrated by Timothy Bush

Clarion Books • New York

Clarion Books • a Houghton Mifflin Company imprint • 215 Park Avenue South, New York, NY 10003

Text copyright © 2002 by Eve Bunting • Illustrations copyright © 2002 by Timothy Bush

The illustrations were executed in watercolor. • The text was set in 30-point Wade Sans Light.

www.houghtonmifflinbooks.com

Printed in Singapore

Library of Congress Cataloging-in-Publication Data

Bunting, Eve

Christmas cricket / by Eve Bunting : illustrated by Timothy Bush.

p. cm.

Summary: On Christmas Eve a little cricket finds its way into a house where its singing is thought to be the voice of an angel.

ISBN 0-618-06554-7

[1. Crickets—Fiction. 2. Christmas—Fiction.] I. Bush, Timothy, ill. II. Title.

PZ7.B91527 Chj 2002   [E]—dc21   2001055266

TWP 10 9 8 7 6 5 4 3 2 1

To the Christmas choir in my garden. You sing like angels.
—E. B.

To my family.
—T. B.

It was cold in the garden. Cricket felt small and worthless in the bigness of night.

He hopped up steps . . .

under a door . . .

. . . and into a kitchen.

He jump-jumped across
something, cold as frozen snow,

skid-skidded across
somewhere, slippery as pond ice,

and onto a place soft
and fresh as grass.

Cricket hop-hopped
around
and into
and out of things
and over to a tall tree
with stars clinging to it.

He jumped onto a low branch,
hid himself,
and began a song.

"Dad? I thought I heard the angel sing," a small voice said, so close that it scared Cricket into silence.

What should he do?
He must not be found.
Should he jump?
Should he try to get away?
Should he stay hidden?

"I thought I heard singing, too."
This was a bigger voice.
A finger gently swung his branch.

What was happening?
Cricket felt dizzy.
He held on tight.
Around him everything
swayed
and jangled
and chimed.

The swinging stopped.

"Did you know that angels
sing in the songs of birds,
and frogs
and people
and crickets?"
the big voice asked,

a voice so gentle that it
calmed Cricket's pounding heart.

"I didn't know that," the little voice said.

Angels sing in the voices of crickets?

Cricket didn't know that, either.
He was small, then.
But not worthless.
What a great discovery!

"Shall we sing with the angel?" the big voice asked.

"Yes, please."

Together the two sang
"Joy to the World."

And in his hiding place
Cricket rubbed his wings,
one against the other,
for his own joy,

and sang
and sang,

and sang.